BROWN SUNSHINE
OF SAWDUST VALLEY

MARGUERITE HENRY

ILLUSTRATED BY **BONNIE SHIELDS**

Aladdin Paperbacks

ALSO BY
MARGUERITE HENRY:

Misty of Chincoteague
A NEWBERY HONOR BOOK

King of the Wind
WINNER OF THE NEWBERY MEDAL

Sea Star: Orphan of Chincoteague

Born to Trot

Brighty of the Grand Canyon

Justin Morgan Had a Horse
A NEWBERY HONOR BOOK

Black Gold

Stormy: Misty's Foal

White Stallion of Lipizza

Mustang: Wild Spirit of the West

San Domingo: The Medicine Hat Stallion

Misty's Twilight

First Aladdin Paperbacks edition May 1998

Text copyright © 1996 by Marguerite Henry
Illustrations copyright © 1996 by Bonnie Shields

Aladdin Paperbacks
An imprint of Simon & Schuster Children's Publishing Division
1230 Avenue of the Americas
New York, NY 10020

Also available in a Simon & Schuster Books for Young Readers edition.
Designed by Leslie Tane
The text of this book was set in 11 point Baskerville Book.
The illustrations are rendered in pencil.
Printed and bound in the United States of America
10 9 8 7 6 5 4 3 2 1

The Library of Congress has cataloged the hardcover edition
as follows:
Henry, Marguerite, 1902-
Brown sunshine of Sawdust Valley / by Marguerite Henry.
p.   cm.
Summary: Molly wants a horse of her own, but when her father's
mare gives birth to a mule, Molly changes her mind and raises the
newborn.
ISBN 0-689-80364-8 (hardcover)
1. Mules—juvenile fiction. [1. Mules—Fiction.] I. Title
PZ10.3.H43Bt 1996 [Fic]—dc20 96-21663 CIP AC
ISBN 0-689-84523-5 (pbk.)

BROWN SUNSHINE
OF SAWDUST VALLEY

To Susan Ambrose—
May this book be a reminder to you
of the gifts you are giving the world.

M . H .

CONTENTS

CHAPTER 1

ALL I WANT TO DO IS RIDE   1

CHAPTER 2

MY TENTH BIRTHDAY   5

CHAPTER 3

HORSE SALE–LOWER BARN   8

CHAPTER 4

NUMBER THIRTEEN   18

CHAPTER 5

I'M HERE NOW   23

CHAPTER 6

I RIDE HER EASY   28

CHAPTER 7

NO TIME TO LOSE   33

CHAPTER 8

GOLDEN IN THE SUNLIGHT   40

CHAPTER 9

LATE AFTERNOON OF THE NEWBORN   46

CHAPTER 10

THE LONER DOWN THE HILL   49

CHAPTER 11
KEEP YOUR TRACES TIGHT!   53

CHAPTER 12
IT'S NOT HOW LONG THE EARS ARE . . .   59

CHAPTER 13
ROYAL GIFT   64

CHAPTER 14
BROWN SUNSHINE GROWS   70

CHAPTER 15
THE TALE OF BROWN SUNSHINE'S TAIL   73

CHAPTER 16
THE COMMITTEE ARRIVES   77

CHAPTER 17
PREPARATIONS   82

CHAPTER 18
SPRING SHOW MULE CLIP   85

CHAPTER 19
MULE DAY   88

CHAPTER 20
THE KING   90

CHAPTER 21
HOME   98

BROWN SUNSHINE
OF SAWDUST VALLEY

CHAPTER 1

ALL I WANT
TO DO IS RIDE

September 1

Dear Diary,

I get a sick feeling whenever I look at a person riding a horse and acting so smug and happy at being up there. I just want to crawl under a rock and cry.

That's why I detest Freddy Westover. Besides owning show horses, he's the fastest forward and the highest scorer on our soccer team. And in school parades he gets to lead the band. But worst of all, he wins the blue ribbons at the horse shows on a big Tennessee walking horse named Strolling Joe.

Me? In soccer they call me P.F., for personal fouls, because I forget to trap or kick the ball. I use my hands instead, so the other team is always getting free kicks. And the only time I get to ride a horse is when Freddy lets me—but it's never on Strolling Joe. It's always on his old mare, Della, who can hardly move because of arthritis.

And he acts like a king granting a favor to his lowest subject. "Molly," he says, "you can ride *once* around the field on Della. Then you can muck out her stall and clean Joe's tack."

Funny thing is, I do exactly what Freddy says, because I just want to ride. It's all I ever think about. Even now when I'm writing in my diary I get all choked up, like I have an allergy or something.

The only good thing about Freddy is his big blue weimaraner dog, Smokestack. He spends more time with me than he does with Freddy, and I think that makes Freddy mad.

One good person in my life is our librarian, Elizabeth Potts. She puts aside horse books for me. I read two a week, even though they're mostly about horse-sick kids who always get a horse at the end of the story. Not like me! And here I live in Tennessee—practically the horse capital of the whole world.

I can't talk to my parents. They have enough to worry about. I hear them talking serious at night about "making ends meet" and wishing they could buy me this or that. But they never mention a horse.

Mom just put on her new CD of "Lights Out." Guess whenever I hear it, I'll fall right asleep wherever I am.

* * *

With a tiny brass key, Molly locked her diary, tucked it under her pillow, and curled up in bed. But she didn't fall right asleep. She pretended she was a famous author and had just sold a book to the movies for a million dollars. Without a second thought, she knew what to do with the money. She'd buy a horse ranch. There'd be a stallion for *every* mare. There'd be two colts, a suckling and a weanling, tagging at each mare's heels. And kids who didn't have horses could come and ride. Nobody would be kept out except Freddy Westover. Or if he ever did show up, he'd have to ride the oldest, slowest horse in the bunch.

For almost a month Molly made no entry in her diary. Then on October first she started a fresh page.

CHAPTER 2

MY TENTH BIRTHDAY

October 1

Dear Diary,

It's a miracle! It's going to happen! Tomorrow is my tenth birthday and Pops is taking me to a horse sale at Lawton's Stock Farm on Duck River near Williamsport. He just sold his old tractor for twice its value to an antique dealer who was passing by and spotted it as a great find. If there is a

young horse, not too expensive, he's mine. Just
like that!

I've got one all pictured in my mind. He's
young and strong. I don't care whether it's a filly or
a boy colt, just so long as it's faster than Della. A
weanling would be about perfect. And it doesn't
matter if he's a Tennessee walking horse or an
American saddlebred or a big Clydesdale with
feathers on his feet. I don't care about color

because Freddy says a good horse can NEVER be a bad color. I guess the only particulars are that he has to be young and able to move . . . fast. I can train him so he'll be absolutely gentle and true blue and will leave his stall for a cross-country jaunt the way I burst out of school at the 3:30 bell.

For Mom's sake, the first thing I'll teach him is to pull a cart so she can deliver her homemade jams and jellies. And by the time he's three, he'll be our do-it-all horse. Wheeee! Tomorrow I'll be

Molly Moore

Horse owner.

P.S. Tomorrow night I'll have LOTS to tell.

CHAPTER 3

HORSE SALE—
LOWER BARN

It was the perfect autumn day in middle Tennessee—trees showing their colors, squirrels scampering off, their cheeks bulging with hickory nuts and persimmons. And along the dry roadsides ragweed flowers tossing their pollen to the wind.

Molly's father whipped out his handkerchief to cover a steam-whistle sneeze. In spite of his hay fever, he was in high spirits. A tall-built man, his red thatch of hair touched the roof of the pickup. He and Molly were barreling along the highway to Williamsport, leaving home and Sawdust Valley far behind.

"For six years I've wanted this day to happen,"

he said. "But all good things take time."

Molly wanted to squeeze her father's hand, but one was holding the wheel and the other clutched a wet handkerchief.

"Will you care," he asked, "whether the animal we can afford is a gelding or a mare?"

"Not even if he's a stallion, Pops," Molly said.

Her father's laughter boomed through the truck. "You're safe there, Punkin, we could never afford a stallion."

For the rest of the ride, they were lost in their own dreams. Molly saw herself riding her dashing

young horse as they led a grand parade, while Pops pictured himself handing over the lead rope of a beautiful yearling to Molly on her tenth birthday.

By the time they found a parking space and Molly had stumbled over tree roots and squawking chickens, the visiting auctioneer had taken his place opposite a tier of homemade bleachers. They were filled to the loft with city folk from Nashville and who knows where else. Sitting alongside were farmers, merchants, and folks from roundabout.

The auctioneer lifted his bowler hat with a flourish and said, "Top o' the mornin', ladies and gentlemen."

Molly looked around. There was only one lady in the audience. She and Molly exchanged smiles.

The auctioneer cupped one hand about his mouth.

"Bring in that strapping big colt," he said in a whisper everyone could hear. From around the side of the barn, a tall boy stepped into the ring leading a frisky colt with a #1 slapped on his rump.

As the boy turned the dancing colt to face the audience, Molly noticed that his whiskers were beaded white as if he'd just been nursing. She caught her breath at the golden-red newness of him.

"Now this feller's already been haltered, as you horse folk can tell; meet Numero Uno."

Molly leaned forward eagerly. It was all she could do to remain in her seat.

"If 'tweren't due to problems of will-probating, the owners'd never sell a strapping fellow like this'un."

Molly nudged Pops. "The colt looked right at me. *At me!*"

"This big little feller is outen a saddlebred mare and a Morgan sire. Who'll start the bidding? At fifty dollars! Make it fifty!"

Molly nudged her father again. "Can we afford him?"

"Only one way to find out. Ten dollars!" he offered.

The auctioneer's voice sneered. "Ten dollars?" he repeated, curling his lips. Suddenly his mood changed. His pace quickened, words slurred. "Who'll make it fifty? Fifty . . . fifty?"

"Twenty-five dollars," piped a little old sun-burned man.

"Pops, bid!"

"Twenty-five, I'm bid. Twenty-five, I'm bid. Who'll make it fifty?"

"Forty!" The woman's voice.

Pops let out one of his ragweed sneezes. The auctioneer smiled his approval, accepting the sneeze as a fifty-dollar bid.

"Oh, Pops, thank you!"

"The gentleman and his little redheaded colleen bid fifty dollars for this strapping young colt that's ready to be trained their way. His sire and dam both were showstoppers . . . with dash 'n' style. He'll win enough blue ribbons to cover the walls of the little girl's bedroom. Make it a hundred, and he's yours."

ALL BIDS ARE FINAL

The auctioneer winked one eye at Molly.

"Sixty." The woman's voice.

Pops fingered the seventy dollars in his pocket and offered it all. "*Seventy dollars!*" he announced with a note of finality.

The sunburned old man snapped his fingers: "Hun-derd!" He seemed ready to bid on and on.

"The gentleman bids one hundred dollars."

"One hundred and twenty-five." The lady's voice interrupted.

"One-fifty." The sunburned man.

"One-fifty. Do I hear one-seventy-five?"

The barn went silent except for a tiny squeal from the colt, pulling toward the open door, as if anxious to be reunited with his mother.

"Going . . . going . . . gone!"

Molly watched the colt being led out of the ring while the elderly man, now sprightly as a grasshopper, hurried off to claim him.

Pops put his arm about Molly.

"There'll be other entries, well-trained; this one was really too green for us!"

"Too green?" Molly repeated. "Oh, Pops, he looked just right to me!"

Horses numbered two through twelve came and went, all ages, all breeds. Each time, the seventy dollars in Mr. Moore's pocket served only to spur the bidding. After a while, Molly's hopes turned to bewilderment. "Pops, can't we do something? Can't we get that foal there to stumble and want to come back?"

"It's too late, Molly. His handler is taking him away." Pops put his hand on Molly's shoulder.

By the time #13 entered the ring, the crowd had

begun thinning out, but still the auction limped on.

"Ladies and Gentlemen, Lady Sue, Number Thirteen, is last and luckiest." The auctioneer warmed to his few bidders. "Meet Lady Sue. She has good years left. Her legs are sounder than a dollar. Not a blemish. Mebbe she's gaunted up a bit, but good hay and oats and lots of TLC will make her a fine, dependable mount to hack across country, jump fallen logs, and show off like the hunter-jumper she is. Fact is, she's half Arab, half Thoroughbred and has been trained as a three-gaited saddle horse. She could be just the ticket for the young redhead sitting with her daddy."

To Molly's surprise, she watched her father go down from the top bench to examine the mare's teeth. Almost immediately he gave a satisfied nod and returned to his seat.

"Who'll offer seventy dollars?" the auctioneer asked with a wink, "for this Thoroughbred with a pedigree longer'n my arm?"

Pops waited for someone else to open the bidding.

"Twenty-five," said a voice with a laugh in it, "for the flea-bitten sorrel."

The silence in the emptying barn made the buzzing of a greenhead fly seem noisy.

"Please, Pops, let's go home!" Molly whispered. But her father didn't hear. He had a rapt expression on his face. He seemed anxious to challenge the bid.

"Who'll offer seventy dollars?"

Pops nodded.

The stands were almost empty. Molly covered her face with her hands. The auctioneer seemed in a hurry to close the bidding.

"I have seventy. I have seventy. Going . . . going . . . gone for seventy dollars to the gentlemen and the young lady, who now own a sensible mount, without any colty tricks. And not a scar on knee or hock."

Molly winced. She had told everybody at school that she was going to get a young horse on her birthday, and it would be as elegant as Secretariat.

"Oh, Pops, why did you do it? This old mare is a shadow of what we both wanted."

"Molly, we can work magic on her. Good food,

good grooming, and plain old believing in her. Let's get that mane and tail combed out, and give her lots of love and we'll transform her in no time."

Molly tried to smile at her father, but she was filled with dismay. Would her friends see Pop's point of view?

CHAPTER 4

NUMBER THIRTEEN

Molly's father chuckled softly as he drove the pickup with the trailer attached through the gate and onto the blacktop road.

"I can't believe it!" he said, reaching for Molly's hand and squeezing it in a clasp so firm it made her blink. "How can we be so lucky? Only seventy dollars for such a well-bred mare! Molly, did you notice her delicate head? Her dish-faced profile? And her small ears? And her tail set on high? And her eyes wide apart?"

The questions stopped suddenly. Pops searched his daughter's face. "Molly! You're crying!"

"Probably it's the ragweed, Pops." Molly broke free of her father's hand and rummaged in her pocket for a handkerchief.

"Poor Molly!" he said. "Isn't it enough you've inherited my red hair and now my hay fever, too? Well, have a good blow, Punkin, you don't have to talk now. Maybe I've said too much."

The pickup left the blacktop, turning out onto the dusty back road to Sawdust Valley. Her father scratched his back against the seat. "All during my growing years, Molly, my folks had nothing but mongrel horses."

She tried to listen, tried to forget the fuzzy Number One colt with the curly tail that looked like a wisp of yarn.

"By mongrel I mean they weren't Belgians or Clydesdales or Percherons; they were just every-day workhorses that slow-footed their way through the fields, combing them into furrows. As a twerp of a boy, stumbling along behind the horses, I used to pass the time picking out cloud shapes in the sky and looking sharp for meadow larks' nests in the furrows of grass."

Molly watched a hawk thunderbolt out of a cloud, sending a covey of quail scattering.

"And on Sundays," Pops confided, "I tried to ride the critters, all free of their everyday collars and harness, but there was no fun in it. Not for them, nor for me. They just shambled along as if they were still pulling a plow."

"I know about slow rides, Pops. I've ridden Freddy's Della, and it's hard to stay awake on her back." Molly tried to keep up her end of the conversation, but she felt squeezed out and small, as if this were not her birthday at all.

"'Course you do, but now we own an elegant

mare, as different from Della as a gazelle from a bull. I know she doesn't look like much right now, but she's a completely different make and model from Della."

"Did she have young teeth, Pops?"

"Well not exactly baby nippers, Molly, but if I'm any judge, the jagged edges can be filed smooth and they'll make very efficient tools for grinding her oats and hay into a healthy mash. Then you just watch how she'll fill out, and how she'll travel."

Molly gave a heavy sigh of resignation.

"Will she go faster than Freddy's Della?"

"Never having ridden old Della, I wouldn't know, but I've a hunch our Lady Sue can fly fast enough to satisfy your old Pops." He took a deep breath. "I can't wait to have a whole Sunday with Lady Sue, and the land and the Lord, and a cooling wind blowing her mane in my face."

Molly was long in answering. She sat stewing, looking dead ahead. So that was it. Lady Sue was to be her father's horse—not hers. He wanted and needed a horse as much or more than she did.

"And when I've tested her gaits for smoothness and her disposition on the trail and in traffic, then she'll be yours. All yours. You won't mind sharing her with your old Pops for just one day of each week, will you?"

To which Molly could only say, "'Course not, Dad." But the words stumbled around the lump in her throat.

Molly and her father sighed in unison, each for a different reason.

CHAPTER 5

I'M HERE NOW

The Moores' house in Sawdust Valley was a modest frame dwelling on three acres of land. The only outbuilding was an old shed that had been unused for years. Lady Sue settled into the shed as if it had been built for her. She didn't seem homesick, or frisky, either. Even when Molly turned her out into the pasture.

Except when she was eating, Lady stood so still she might have been in a museum. She didn't object to the vet who came to rasp her teeth or the blacksmith who came to trim her feet or the leg rubbings and poultices Mr. Moore gave her.

Dr. Bill Winquist commented on her "quiet demeanor." "Usually, I have to use a twitch to distract a horse while I file its teeth."

The blacksmith made almost the same comment. "Appears she ain't worn shoes in a devil of a time. Yet she ain't skittish. Most always when feet has been neglected, I got to give the lip a good twist to tone down the kickin'. Do you want I should shoe her, front *and* back?"

"Yes, four new shoes," Mr. Moore said, proud

of his new mare. But Molly wondered if Lady had any spunk at all!

Freddy Westover came over to watch the shoeing. Smokestack trotted up a few minutes later, taking a spot right beside Molly. He sniffed at the pieces of hoof lying on the ground—they were too tempting to resist.

"She's o-l-d," Freddy stretched out the word. "She'll end up a flea-bitten gray."

"I like grays," Molly snapped. Suddenly she felt old, too. Freddy had that effect on her. He could always make her feel stupid.

"She'll probably end up a roan," Mr. Moore said with authority. "And I wager she won't flinch at anything. What Molly and I care about is performance, not color."

Freddy left before the end of the shoeing. When all four of Lady Sue's hooves had bright new shoes, Molly's father paid the blacksmith. Then, bridling the mare, he swung his leg over her back and settled into position. He clucked and jiggled the reins.

Like a barn swallow in flight, Lady Sue wheeled

and with a soaring motion was up, up, and away. Mr. Moore looked excited—like a little kid. Molly stared after them, pleased with her father's happiness but even more astounded at Lady's eagerness. Pops gave a commanding whoa—and Lady willingly stopped. He walked over to Molly and, almost bowing, he handed the reins to her. For the first time, Molly felt a flutter of excitement.

Do I want to ride her bareback? Molly thought. I'll stick to bareback, since Pops already rides her without a saddle and she is fine like that. Pops is much bigger than I am! She might behave differently with my weight.

Molly led Lady Sue easily to the fence. The horse stood very still while Molly climbed the rails and mounted. Lady didn't even move as Molly settled onto her back. And who should show up at that very moment but Freddy on Strolling Joe. Lady was immediately aware of them. She let out a whinny as if to say "I'M HERE NOW."

Freddy sneered. "Molly! Does the old mare know how to walk?"

Molly clicked to Lady, and instead of a walk she broke into a trot! It took Strolling Joe's fastest walk to catch up with her. Freddy's expression was kindled with surprise, and while Molly held fast to Lady's mane, she suddenly felt a burst of pride at being her owner!

CHAPTER 6

I RIDE HER EASY

November

Dear Diary,

Gosh, in only a month, Lady Sue's looking so much better. Maybe it's her winter coat coming in. But she doesn't look as skinny as when we first brought her home. Although she's not my Dream Horse, she's more fun than I expected.

Last night at supper, Mom, who shies away from horses as if they were dinosaurs, admitted that even *she* could see a change in Lady.

"I'm so proud of you and Daddy," she said. "It's one thing to buy a fine horse to begin with, but to take an aged mare and restore her to a kind of elegance . . . well, that must be what

your manual calls horsemanship."

You know, Diary, I think Mom's right. Old horses need almost as much care as foals. I mean, it doesn't take anything for Freddy to make Strolling Joe look good. That horse is only four years old and just looks good naturally. But with Lady . . . the sunken places above her eyes are becoming less noticeable and she's starting to look more filled out. Even distinguished.

Besides, today when Strolling Joe was doing

his fastest running walk, Lady, at her fastest trot, easily kept pace with him.

Pops rides Lady only on Sundays. All week I have her for my very own. Day after day, we move through autumn stillness or whirling winds. And when it rains, I spend the afternoon in the shed, reading aloud to her from *My Friend Flicka* or one of our equitation books.

Mostly, though, she prefers the rain-sloshed pasture to my stories. She dashes out and lets the raindrops trickle down her back.

It's like the manual says, "Horses have got to live their own lives. Only rarely do they share their inner feelings."

All of our lives have changed . . . because of Lady. Mom is really in business now! She's making twice as many jellies and jams as before. And Lady is pulling a cart full of tart-smelling currants and sweet red raspberries, and strawberry rhubarb preserves, apricots with almonds, blue plum, ginger marmalade, rose-geranium jelly, spiced grape jelly, and blueberry jam.

Mom's even become adventurous; she's made

a new blend using five different fruits. This was the end result of two weeks of experimenting. Pops and I got used to seeing everything but the kitchen sink simmering away on the stove. Acorns, nasturtium leaves, sassafras roots (that *I* had to dig up), and dandelion stems boiling away and sending their particular smells into the steamy kitchen. Only one new jam came of these long days of experimenting. Now orders come in daily for it. Mom calls it "Fabulous Five Fruit Medley." I think helping with the household expenses makes Mom feel happier about everything.

Pops has changed, too. He even looks younger. He went to a new doctor who gave him pills that put an end to his sneezing and wheezing. Often when he rides Lady bareback, people ask him if he used to be a trainer, or a jockey. He breaks into a big grin and his face gets red.

I ride Lady Sue after school to keep her in shape. I ride her easy, thinking about her age. But she never pulls toward home even when we get close. She passes by our drive as if she's just getting warmed up and wants to go on.

At bedtime, I don't hear worried voices talking about me anymore. The light under Mom and Pops's bedroom door goes out earlier, letting me write in my diary until I'm ready for sleep. I don't even toss and turn. We're all too tired and happy, thanks to Lady Sue!

CHAPTER 7

NO TIME TO LOSE

Most of the neighbor kids ate lunch at the school cafeteria, but Molly hurried home every day to feed and water Lady Sue. Mrs. Moore was pleased to have Molly at home, even though it was Lady who claimed most of Molly's attention. Only after the mare's pail of water had been freshened and the measure of oats poured into her manger was Molly ready to wash up at the kitchen sink and sit down to her own bowl of soup and a peanut butter sandwich.

Mrs. Moore usually remained standing at the door after Molly left again for school. It was a relief that Molly had grown to accept Lady Sue. "There are times," Mrs. Moore thought aloud, "when all's right with Molly, then all's right with my world!"

She turned back to the kitchen, singing a hymn in her Sunday voice. She did up the dishes and put them away, still humming. Then she picked up a magazine from the sideboard and went upstairs to her bedroom to read. A whole blessed hour of peace!

Before getting comfortable in her recliner, she lowered the window shade against the blinding sunlight streaming onto her magazine. In one glance she saw Lady in the pasture thrashing and rolling from side to side. The magazine dropped to the floor. For a second the mare lay still, but her body seemed bloated as if it might explode.

Colic! The word froze, unspoken in Mrs. Moore's mind.

Panic. What to do? Nothing must happen to

the mare now, just when Molly had grown to love her.

There was no mistaking the mare's symptoms. Words of advice said themselves, right out of the manual. "When you suspect colic, call your vet at once. No time to lose."

Mrs. Moore wished Pops were home. He'd know what to do. And wouldn't waste time. There was no use *her* trying to help Lady Sue—she didn't know anything about horses. She had to get Doc Winquist. *Now!*

Nervous fingers dialed the phone.

Click. Click. Click. So many numbers. Click. Click. Click. Click.

And the canned words. "Please check with your operator for the correct number. The number you have dialed is not in service at this time."

Mrs. Moore hung up and dialed "0."

"Operator, please dial for me. Our mare needs a vet immediately. She may have the colic."

The clicks sounded foreboding. Strange.

Then Bzz. Bzz. Bzz.

"Sorry, ma'am, the line's busy."

What now? I'll have to go get Doc Winquist! He's got to save Molly's mare.

The white Chevy is with Pops. The only thing I have is the old pickup, which seems to run only when it wants to. There! It coughed a bit. Hurray! It started.

Through mud holes, onto hard roads Mrs. Moore steered the rattling truck, blowing her horn before even crossing the iron bridge and crunching into Doc Winquist's yard. She slammed on the brakes, sending chickens and geese flapping.

Mrs. Winquist hurried outside. "Florence Moore!" she exclaimed. "What brings you out this way in such a hurry, honking and scaring my chickens?"

"Our mare is down with the colic. Your line was busy, and I just couldn't wait. Is Doc home?"

"Sorry. Jensen's show horse got tangled in barbed wire and Bill went to sew him up. He's been gone near two hours, but maybe I can reach him by phone."

"Okay. Tell him I'll pick him up. It'd be out of

his way to come back home when we can take the shortcut to Sawdust Valley."

When Mrs. Moore arrived at the neighbor's farm a few minutes later, Doc Winquist, black bag in hand, stood at the gate waiting for the pickup to grind to a stop.

He opened the truck door and set his bag on the floor. All in one breath he said, "Now compose yourself, Florence, and tell me all the symptoms so I can be ready to go to work soon as we get there."

Her foot bearing down on the gas pedal, Mrs. Moore explained as the old pickup crow-hopped along. "Molly loves this gentle mare. And I saw her rolling and thrashing in the pasture."

"Yes, go on."

"First time Molly's had a horse of her own. And now, just when everything is getting so perfect, the mare could die."

"We'll not let her die. Colic isn't always a killer. It can be just a stomach ache. Has the mare been wormed regularly?"

"Yes, I'm sure of it."

"Good! Has she been overeating?"

"I don't think so. But her barrel did look bloated."

"It could be a gas pocket. Horses can't burp like people, so they get down and roll. Or . . ."

"Or what?"

"Or poor teeth sometimes cause indigestion. Oh, any number of things. Now I tell you what . . ."

The whine of a police siren interrupted him.

"Guess you're speeding, Florence. Pull over and let me do the talking."

The officer got out of his car and slow-footed to the pickup. "Fire someplace?" he drawled.

"Yes, Officer," the doctor said. "A mare with colic must feel like she's swallowed a firebomb. I'm Doc Winquist, the vet."

The officer pinched off his sarcasm. He nodded to Mrs. Moore and shook hands with the doctor.

"I once lost a good saddlebred mare to the colic," the officer said. "She had a twisted gut. Died because I couldn't get a vet soon enough."

"Oh, Officer . . ."

"Now, lady, don't go jumpin' to conclusions. My horse was getting on in years."

"So is our mare," wailed Mrs. Moore.

The officer stuffed his pencil and pad into his pocket. "We're wastin' time," he said. "Follow me."

Siren screaming, the police car shot ahead to lead the way, as traffic melted into the distance.

CHAPTER 8

GOLDEN IN
THE SUNLIGHT

Molly's school bus pulled into the Moores' driveway just as the police car and the pickup roared ahead in a cloud of dust. Molly was first to leap out of the bus and run after them as they headed for the pasture.

When Molly saw Doc Winquist, she felt sick. *What could be wrong? Lady Sue was fine when I fed her before I left for school.* But as Molly rounded the corner of the house, she had a full view of the pasture—there was Lady standing up, looking all golden in the sunlight.

A flood of relief washed over Molly. She crawled through the fence with Doc Winquist and the officer close on her heels.

Suddenly they came to a full stop. Lady was standing directly ahead. Her tail was shifted to one side—exposing a bubblelike white bag.

Molly looked closer in terror. What was happening to her mare? Then she saw a tiny hoof stretching inside the white bag of her stomach.

Doc Winquist laughed with relief. "Molly! Why didn't you tell me your mare was in foal?"

Both Molly and her mother gasped in unison. *"But we didn't know!"* Molly's brain whirled with unanswered questions. How could she not have known that Lady was in foal? Who was the sire? What did *he* look like?

Molly and Mrs. Moore stepped back to give Doc Winquist plenty of room to help his patient. Lady Sue put her nose to the ground and started to lie down, then she stood up quickly and changed sides.

"This is okay," Doc Winquist assured them. "She's positioning a safe birth for the foal. Looks like Lady's done this before. That's why you didn't know. I'll bet you thought she was just gaining weight. This often happens with brood mares—and some humans," he added.

In a quick moment, Lady made a complete turn to her other side while a long foreleg and a flattened nose escaped the bag.

The head appeared as Doc Winquist gently stroked the sac away from the dark brown, furry foal. He continued to massage the sac away from the foal's wet face.

"Do all babies have such long ears when they're born?" Molly asked.

"Only if the baby is a mule, Molly. And this one is definitely a mule!"

"A MULE!" Molly gasped in disbelief. What would the rest of her small brown body look like?

In moments the beautiful form of the entire baby appeared, and there was no doubt that it was anything but perfect. "Oh, she's precious and she's *mine!*" Molly cried out.

"Only one problem, Molly," Doc Winquist said. "She is a *he.*"

"I don't care. He's *beautiful!* He's even more beautiful than my Dream Horse."

A crowd of kids from the school bus had gathered around to see the excitement. Doc Winquist was already in charge and the policeman stood with hands on his hips, whistling in amazement.

"How'd you get a mule, Molly?" one of the kids asked.

Freddy Westover closed in, howling in laughter.

"You get a mule when the father is a jack—a donkey! Ha, ha! Molly's got a mule."

Molly tried to gather her thoughts quickly. She didn't want Freddy catching her off guard. "I know, Freddy. I've got eyes!" She watched the sun glistening on the baby's wet coat. "Anyway, I've already got a name for him."

"What is it?" her mother and Freddy and all the kids from the school bus demanded, almost in the same breath. "What's his name?"

Molly took a deep breath to clear her confusion.

"His name is . . ." Her voice stopped only a moment, then picked up with a determined look at Freddy. "His name is . . . *Brown Sunshine of Sawdust Valley!*"

"But he's brown because his coat is still wet from the birthing," Mrs. Moore said.

"I know, I know." Molly ran her fingers over Lady Sue. "She's wet, too. She had her baby all by herself."

Now a white Chevy curved into the yard and skidded to a stop at a respectful distance from the mare, who was nuzzling her baby, licking him from head to tail, identifying him forever as her own.

When he came over and caught sight of the brand-new mule, Mr. Moore bellowed his happiness. "Molly! . . . we each have our own animal now! The baby mule with the handsome ears is all yours!"

The school kids sighed in wonder and envy as they stumbled up the steps of the bus heading for home.

CHAPTER 9

LATE AFTERNOON OF THE NEWBORN

It was almost dark before Sawdust Valley settled down to an evening of quiet—the school bus doors had squeezed shut, with the police car in the lead and Freddy Westover heading for home, throwing his last jibe to Molly.

"Lemme know how much the auctioneer adds on to Lady Sue's price for giving you a freebie mule." With a grin, he mounted his bicycle, made a double salute to Molly's mother and father, and winged his way homeward.

Dr. Winquist led Lady Sue with her wobbling baby to the stable.

"So," he said, "you really didn't suspect Lady Sue was in foal?"

"We had no idea, Doc Winquist! I guess because Lady was so skinny when we got her, we thought the weight gain was just good food and care."

"He was a complete surprise. That's what makes the little fellow all the more welcome," said Mrs. Moore, "doesn't it, Molly?"

"Exactly!" Molly said. She was stroking Sunshine with her fingertips. The foal wriggled out of reach and out of step.

Soon his feet felt the touch of fresh straw, and he fell to his knees with an audible sigh. The watchers grinned one to the other in shared envy. Even the mare sighed.

Only Mr. Moore had a worry. "I wonder why the auctioneer didn't tell us that Lady was in foal."

Doc Winquist answered, "Maybe he thought it would add a great deal to her cost. Or maybe it would kill the sale for people who don't like mules, or double the price for people who do. Or maybe he just didn't know."

"Still, we don't have the jack's history," Mr. Moore said with a frown. "His owner might pop up and bother us for a great sum of money—if Brown Sunshine ever wins at a mule show in Nashville or out in California or right here in Columbia, Tennessee."

Mrs. Moore solved everything. "Let's leave that for another day. Right now, Molly is ready to warm some bran mash that she made this morning for Lady Sue, and Doc Winquist is anxious to get a ride home after a long day. Pops is happy to drive him, as he has a string of questions to ask about caring for the baby mule."

"And what will you be doing, Mrs. Moore?" the vet asked, laughing.

"I'll be fixing a fine dinner for Molly and her father—the proud owners of a newborn with long elegant ears!"

CHAPTER 10

THE LONER
DOWN THE HILL

Dear Diary,

I'm glad I wasn't home until the *good* news! I would have been terrified seeing Lady rolling from side to side on the ground. Poor Mom! But she really handled it well, burning up the road all the way to Doc's place, then to the Jensens', then back. And what a surprise! What they thought was colic was Brown Sunshine ready to be born.

The first two nights I slept in the stable with Brown Sunshine and Lady Sue. I couldn't believe Mom and Pops let me! They actually suggested it—*if* I had Freddy's weimaraner Smokestack on guard.

Even though Smokestack belongs to Freddy, he used to come over on his own if ever Lady Sue or I needed him. Now Smoke is feeling more important than ever with a brand-new creature to watch over. It's unbelievable how gentle an eighty-pound weimaraner can be! He sniffed and snuffed his way slowly toward the stable as if he knew there was guard work to do. And then he sniffed and snuffed Brown Sunshine from head to tail. And Lady Sue let him do it! Now,

that alone is proof that Smokestack is special.

He has practically taken up residence in Sunshine's barn. They've become great buddies, playing chase and making up their own games. And every once in a while Freddy comes over to see what's going on. Of course, he never joins in the fun. He stands there, making rude comments about how ugly or dumb mules are. Just because he has show horses, he thinks he's better!

Something else unusual is happening. Our neighbor, the man who lives down the hill, keeps peering over his fence at Brown Sunshine. He only has one arm. He lost the other a few years ago in a traffic accident. His wife was killed in that same accident.

His name is Joe Henry Covington, at least that's the name tacked onto one of his fence posts. But we've called him "the loner" ever since Christmas, when Mom brought him a loaf of homemade bread and a jar of Fabulous Five Fruit Medley. He accepted them gratefully enough, but hurried back into his house, as if he preferred to be alone. Rarely does he speak to anyone. He never paid any attention to us until Brown Sunshine was born. Now he's at the fence every day . . . watching.

I wish that Freddy had never said anything about Brown Sunshine being a freebie mule. I can't help worrying that the owners of the jack are going to turn up and ask us for money . . . or take Brown Sunshine away.

There's Mr. Covington again. I keep wondering: What is he thinking? Why is he so interested? Does he know something we don't?

CHAPTER 11

KEEP YOUR
TRACES TIGHT!

Brown Sunshine with the sensitive ears and the bouncy tail grew to enjoy the sameness of his days. Early each morning the sun woke him, warming his coat first and then his bones underneath.

Along with the rising sun, Molly sang herself out of the house and gave Brown Sunshine an affectionate swat on the rump.

"Mornin', Sunshine," she said. "Time to be up and at 'em." Brown Sunshine had no idea what the words meant, but they had a friendly encouraging sound, and he answered with a bawl that turned into a squeal and ended in a long whicker.

This let Smokestack know that it was time to

run over to the feeder for a quick game of tug-of-war with the oat hay that Molly would give Sunshine for breakfast. Molly loved this game. It had quickly become a celebration of each morning. What a sight—a mule and a dog tugging fiercely at a mouthful of hay. Once Brown Sunshine had tugged so hard that Smoke went flying through the air and did a complete somersault before landing again!

Molly laughed. "You two should be in a circus!"

All of a sudden one morning, Mr. Covington, who had been watching Brown Sunshine keenly, came striding up the hill.

Molly stood frozen, shocked by his presence, feeling that he must have come for her mule. *He must be here to take Brown Sunshine away*! she thought wildly.

"Is your father here?" he said on his arrival. "I'd like to talk to him before he leaves this morning."

Molly was so nervous that she couldn't answer. But it didn't matter. Mr. Covington had no sooner finished his question, when Pops came out of the house. The two men shook hands, each curious about the other.

Mr. Covington pulled a picture from his pocket showing a handsome buggy pulled by a MULE!

"The mule is yours?" Mr. Moore asked, studying the photograph.

Covington nodded. "Yes, but she passed on."

"Oh, I'm sorry," Pops said. "I had no idea."

Molly's mind was racing. *His mule's dead, and now he wants mine!*

"She died years ago of old age. I raised her from a baby. I'll never have a friend like her again."

Pops nodded. "I understand."

Enough! Molly thought. *What more does he want? I wish he'd go home now to his own side of the fence!*

"I want to offer my buggy for your wife to use in delivering jams and jellies to her customers," Mr. Covington said.

Molly sighed with relief, then quickly covered her mouth as her face turned a bright red. *How could I have been so wrong!* Fortunately, no one was paying any attention to her.

"I sure appreciated getting that fine jam for Christmas," Mr. Covington went on to say.

Molly could hardly believe what was happening. *What an adventure for the animals and for Mom! She might sell twice as much from a snappy buggy surrounded by three proud animals—an elegant mare, her darling baby mule, and a proud guard dog.*

Molly was caught up in the excitement. "What could I do? I'd sure like to go along," she said.

"We'd make our trip once a week . . . say, on Saturdays," Mr. Covington suggested. "It would be a great help if you'd carry the trays of jams and jellies into the people's houses."

Mr. Moore was still studying the picture. "That's a fine buggy," he said. "My wife will be delighted. The old cart was much too small."

Mr. Covington nodded in agreement. "Right now, the buggy is up on blocks in my barn. But with a little elbow grease, I'll have it ready to roll in no time."

Mrs. Moore came out of the house and joined the excitement. She, too, studied the picture of the buggy and the long-ago couple riding in it. She listened to Mr. Covington's offer. She hugged Molly and actually shook hands with Brown Sunshine, who happened to be lifting his right foreleg and lowering his head to observe a butterfly landing on his leg. Everybody laughed. Even Brown Sunshine snorted, as if he enjoyed shaking hands and having an audience.

"One other thing," Mr. Covington now turned his attention to Molly. "I've been watching your little mule. He's a fine specimen. I worked mules on my farm for almost twenty years, and I sorely miss turning a bit of dirt. If you and your mom have any questions about how to handle Brown Sunshine, I'd like to help out. Truth is, I'm itching to get my good hand on a good mule again."

Molly and her mother smiled and thanked Mr. Covington. As for Mr. Moore, he invited his neighbor to hurry repairs on the buggy. And Mr. Covington did hurry. In two weeks, the buggy was back in shape and the entourage was on its way to sell jams and jellies. At every house where they pulled up, delighted customers ran out with cameras and carrots.

CHAPTER 12

IT'S NOT HOW LONG
THE EARS ARE . . .

Agreat peace settled over Molly's life. The worry over the identity of Brown Sunshine's sire seemed unimportant. Would the people who planned the breeding come to claim Brown Sunshine? Or was it an act of God without any help from man?

The days settled into a joyous routine. Lady Sue blossomed with her Saturday morning trips delivering Mrs. Moore's jams and jellies. Never before had she enjoyed such lively company. Not only her baby mule following or leading the way from house to house, but Smokestack monitoring the procession and barking in approval. Their excitement was contagious! Mrs. Moore grew

happy in the everyday security, and Mr. Covington enthusiastically answered Molly's endless
questions on the raising and training of mules.

To spend more time with Brown Sunshine,
Molly's classroom work improved sharply. Summer vacation was just around the corner and
Molly had convinced Mr. Covington to help
teach Brown Sunshine to pull a plow, or a fine
cart, and the challenge of cross-country riding.

Freddy's was the only negative voice to be
heard. Between horse shows he came over to the
Moores to compare mules to horses: "Mules are
stupid. Mules are slow. Mules are mean and low
class." Whatever Freddy could say to make Molly
feel bad made Freddy feel good. He had *all* the
answers. In her diary, Molly gave Freddy a piece
of her mind.

June sixth, the very first day of summer vacation, Molly woke up early filled with excitement,
as Mr. Covington promised to begin training

Brown Sunshine that very day. Molly helped her mother make jelly and finished her daily chores of cleaning her room and doing the breakfast dishes, so the rest of the day was hers. She would learn how to train Brown Sunshine!

Mr. Covington arrived with halter and lead rope in hand. Molly opened the pasture gate for him. He walked quietly over to Brown Sunshine and gently placed the rope around Sunshine's neck. Then he slid the halter onto his head. Molly helped to fasten the buckle. All the while Mr. Covington spoke in a very calm, low voice. "Easy, boy, it's okay, boy. Whoa there, boy."

Molly watched in awe. Brown Sunshine seemed to understand exactly what Mr. Covington was telling him. All was fine while Mr. Covington held on to the rope and stroked Sunshine's shoulder. Then Mr. Covington gave a tug on the rope for Brown Sunshine to follow him to the gate. Sunshine suddenly pulled away in the opposite direction!

"Whoa, boy! Easy there. Come now," Mr. Covington coaxed. But Brown Sunshine had other plans. Mr. Covington gave a quick, hard jerk on the lead rope, which got Brown Sunshine's full attention. His forelegs spread wide apart as he stopped in his tracks and trembled.

Mr. Covington approached him again with that same calming voice. "Easy, boy, it's okay, come on, boy," he said, and stroked Sunshine's shoulder once more. Then he gave another tug.

Brown Sunshine followed courageously. It could and *did* work!

Molly was delighted to see how smart her mule was. She was even more delighted when she noticed Freddy had been standing behind her and had seen the whole performance. He looked impressed.

Freddy said, "Mister, how did you get him to follow, when mules are known for their stubbornness?"

"Well, son," Mr. Covington replied. "It's not how long the ears are—it's what's between them."

CHAPTER 13

ROYAL GIFT

Dear Diary,

Twenty whole months have passed! Brown Sunshine sure has grown and no longer looks like a fuzzy baby. But he is still just as beautiful!

He's beginning to learn the lifestyle of a growing mule. He's listening to Mr. Covington's lessons on "ground driving." Because of his one arm, Mr. Covington is teaching Brown Sunshine to work with only one line, the jerk-line. Mr. Covington is also teaching him to carry a small saddle, sometimes an old Army or McClellan saddle, or two potato sacks to get him used to weight on his back.

Even Freddy Westover is "coming around." He won't admit it to me, but I can tell from the way

he talks about Mr. Covington and Brown Sunshine. Watching a true muleteer at work is changing his opinion of mules. He and Smokestack are spending a lot of time at our house.

I'm in seventh grade now. Today my teacher, Miss Spinks, asked me to stand in front of the class and read my composition entitled MULE DAY IN COLUMBIA, TENNESSEE.

"The class will please close all books," she said, with an eye on Freddy, "and give close attention to Molly's speech."

My knees started to quake till I got a good look at Freddy in the back row. At first Freddy showed his usual smirk. But then he was listening without a sneer, as if he was interested.

Miss Spinks peered over her half-glasses. "I want the entire class to see how Molly takes a subject she has researched at the library and makes a fine story of it, with a beginning, a middle, and an ending."

I owe a lot of thanks to our librarian, Miss Potts, who helped me with my essay. I can still see her stacking a pile of books on how General George Washington brought mules to America, and how certain cities held King Mule celebrations that attracted thousands of admirers from all over the United States and Canada. She even brought a roll of newspapers flashing pictures of past Mule Day parades. As the stack of material grew higher and higher, the researchers sitting beside me wrinkled their noses in envy. But as I studied the Crowning, I could easily imagine Brown Sunshine being crowned King Mule.

Gulping, I began, "For 364 days a year, the mule works for man." My voice strengthened. "On the 365th day, man works for the mule. He puts on a celebration for all mules. It's almost as big as the Rose Bowl Parade in California and more important to me because it honors live animals and their work."

The class settled down.

"The reason it's more important," I went on, without even looking at my notes, "is that this festival crowns an animal that has earned his reward, and not just by being beautiful!

"In Columbia, Tennessee," I said with pride, and thinking of Brown Sunshine all the while, "the most typical and beautiful mule is crowned KING before thousands of visitors from all across America."

"Molly," Miss Spinks got up from behind her desk to stand beside me. "I would like to hold up before the class this splendid illustration of your essay."

I wished she hadn't done that, because all the kids were going to figure that I was her pet. I took a deep breath and continued.

"Our first President, General George Washington, made the mule popular in America. When the Revolutionary War ended, and the general returned home, he was shocked by the drabness of his land at Mount Vernon. So he turned his mind to scientific farming. He had heard that 'Spain's enormous Catalonian donkeys sired fine work mules who were greater in size and strength than horses.' Besides, as he put it, 'their cheap keeping was much in their favor.' General Washington tried several times to buy the Spanish donkeys, but with no luck. It was against Spanish law to export jacks.

"The news that the general himself was interested finally reached the King of Spain, who was so honored that he ordered two of the finest jacks in his kingdom to be sent as a gift. Although one died on board ship, the other jack arrived at Mount Vernon in fine fettle.

"Examining the handsome jack standing on the piazza of his mansion one summer morning, General Washington said, 'From him, I hope to secure a race of extraordinary goodness which will stock the country. He is indeed a Royal Gift, and henceforward that will be his name.'

"Within a few years, the general had mated several horse-mares to Royal Gift and gotten some strapping mules. They were so tough that he put them to work at an early age. Friends and neighbors shook their heads in amazement. How fat and sleek the mule kept in spite of his work! How he pulled and plowed and cultivated on the hottest days! They wanted mules, too. And so, before very long, the Virginia countryside was dotted with the long-eared sons and daughters of Royal Gift."

CHAPTER 14

BROWN SUNSHINE
GROWS

Molly's essay was entered in the Tennessee state contest. By the next spring it had won the regional competition and was entered in the statewide finals. Winners wouldn't be announced until school opened in the fall. Molly dared to be hopeful.

Meantime, Brown Sunshine had turned two years old. His training was now more serious. By summer's end, he was doing light work—hauling firewood to clear the Moores' land.

Also, Joe Henry Covington yearned to turn a little dirt himself. He figured that Brown Sunshine was strong enough and ready to plow a garden. Joe Henry even offered his walking plow to give Mrs.

Moore a proper garden tool. But he knew he couldn't drive a green mule and handle the plow at the same time. He needed help, and was delighted when a changed Freddy volunteered.

"It won't be easy," Mr. Covington explained, but Freddy was not convinced. Together they went to work.

Molly was furious. Freddy had taken over *her* mule and *her* job! Mr. Covington hooked Brown Sunshine to the plow. He drove with a single jerk-line while Freddy grabbed the plow handles. This made Brown Sunshine uneasy. After only a few rows, they snagged a root with the blade. A handle flew up in Freddy's face and smacked him under the chin, making him bite his tongue. His world spun—both his chin and tongue were bleeding.

Molly ran to the house and made up her first ice pack. She hurried outdoors to find Mr. Covington holding his red bandanna under Freddy's chin. Mr. Covington took the ice pack, gave it to Freddy, and pointed to a shade tree. "Take this, son, and sit in the shade, over yonder, till the bleeding stops."

Molly eagerly stepped in and took the plow in hand. Mr. Covington picked up the jerk-line and Brown Sunshine trusted Molly so completely that he moved off as if he'd been a plower for years.

The system worked so well that Mr. Covington and Molly formed a business going about the neighborhood, plowing and planting. Even Freddy joined in. He loaded all the equipment—the plow, cultivators, disc, and shovels—onto a big wooden "groundslide" to transport from place to place. Brown Sunshine pulled the slide with great enthusiasm, and the daily work gave an obvious satisfaction to Molly and her mule!

CHAPTER 15

THE TALE OF BROWN SUNSHINE'S TAIL

When school began that fall, it was announced that Molly Moore's essay had won the state competition. Her achievement was published in newspapers across Tennessee. Molly was asked to go to Nashville to read her essay on TV, and to talk to the General Assembly on Youth Day.

Molly and her mule received a lot of attention and publicity for the upcoming Mule Day. The committee in Columbia took notice and discussed Brown Sunshine as King for a Day. For Molly, it all seemed possible, yet incredible. Her mother made a scrapbook of the news articles, and Pops showed it to everyone who came to the house.

Meanwhile, in midwinter, Tennessee experienced a cold snap for an entire week. One night Molly left the stock tank filled with water. She had insulated Brown Sunshine and Lady Sue's stall with extra straw, which helped keep them warmer but didn't stop the water from freezing. As Lady Sue and Brown Sunshine huddled together, Sunshine's beautiful long tail rested in the stock tank. During the long chilling night, he never even felt the clutch of ice forming about his tail.

The next morning, Molly sang her way down to the barn. With a cheerful "Up and at 'em," and a slap on Sunshine's rump, she sent him wriggling forward without his usual freedom. He began squealing in panic.

"What is it, Brown Sunshine? What's wrong?"

Lady Sue was already outside but Sunshine was held fast by something. Molly looked more closely. Her eyes widened. His tail was frozen in the tank!

"No, Sunshine! Don't pull! Wait! I'll help you!"

With one fierce tug, Brown Sunshine escaped

the stall. But he escaped with only half his tail. He shook himself in bewilderment, craning his neck until he finally saw his stub of a tail. It didn't bother him at all! He was free, and ready for breakfast!

"You look so different without your flag of a tail," Molly cried. "How will you show happiness with only half a tail? Will it grow back in time for the King Mule contest? Poor Sunshine!"

Now she heard the school bus coming, so Molly filled a bucket with fresh water and called in Brown Sunshine and his mamma. Lady drank it dry. Molly filled it again but Brown Sunshine refused to drink. He'd had enough of water for the time being, thank you very much! He turned rat-tail bone and went out to the pasture to graze.

CHAPTER 16

THE COMMITTEE ARRIVES

As early as February, the smell of spring tickled Sunshine's nose. At the same time, the Committee for the Columbia Mule Day Celebration decided to inspect Brown Sunshine for the possible role of King Mule. They arrived at the Moores' before eight in the morning and were impressed to see Molly emerging from the stable with a clump of leathers over her shoulder. She was followed by Joe Henry Covington.

The members of the committee had already taken a look at Brown Sunshine grazing in a nearby pasture. One man immediately made his mission clear. "Molly," he said, reaching out to shake hands. "I'm Drew Kent and these are my associates, Dwight Oliver and Shane Bigelow."

Molly, shaking his hand, replied, "Pleased to meet you. This is Mr. Covington. He is training Brown Sunshine and me to be a team."

"Ah, yes," Kent nodded. "Just the man we've been wanting to meet. We've heard how well you know mules and it just so happens we need a Grand Marshal for the parade."

Molly and Mr. Covington grinned in pleasure.

"And we've come to consider Brown Sunshine for the role of King Mule."

Molly sighed. "But Brown Sunshine has just turned three. He's so young. We've actually been working him for only a year."

"His age is no problem at all," Bigelow replied. "In England and other countries, kings are often mere lads."

"Covington," Oliver said, "what the crowd really likes to see is evidence of work done. And Brown Sunshine already has pull-markings over his shoulders, and light markings above his belly. The plain pull-markings are the greatest! They will make up for the shortness of his tail."

"Brown Sunshine is definitely as tall as any work-mule," Drew added. "A King Mule has to be at least fifteen hands at five years, and Brown Sunshine is fifteen hands at three years! And he's twice as handsome. When he's crowned King Mule for a Day, the people will go wild! But I don't suppose mules can really feel a pride rising inside them."

"Why not?" Molly asked. "They show gladness in different ways from humans."

"You bet your boots they do," Joe Henry said, his eyes remembering. "Once when I was in fourth grade, a horse and a mule visited our school. I had sticky hands from just finishing an ice cream cone and the mule licked my fingers long after the ice cream was gone."

"I'd like to nominate Brown Sunshine as our King Mule if we, the committee, agree," said Oliver.

"I do," said Drew.

"Definitely!" Bigelow agreed. "We won't have too long for this committee to fit the jewels into his crown. And only a few weeks to see how the Queen of the Parade takes on her role of crowning so young a king."

"Probably," Drew explained to Molly, "if you had been a few years older, we would have nominated you as Mule Queen! But since you're only thirteen, we want you to be a member of the Court, and ride on the float with Brown Sunshine. Joe Henry Covington will be Grand Marshal."

Molly clapped her hands and Joe Henry laughed. How could they have questioned this great honor for Brown Sunshine? It might never be offered again!

Brown Sunshine snorted a kind of relief when the visitors' car turned out onto the highway. Joe Henry let out a wah-hoo strong enough to be heard by the members of the committee, and to draw a wild honking and hand-waving from their car. Brown Sunshine answered with a half bray, half whinny.

"Molly," Joe Henry said, "it's good we have a month of hard work ahead so we won't go mooning about the glory of the crowning and the people shouting, 'Brown Sunshine! Brown Sunshine!'"

CHAPTER 17

PREPARATIONS

Dear Diary,

Mom and I are in orbit! We've been shopping for a long queenly gown for me to wear to the crowning of Brown Sunshine. The one we finally decided on looks almost like a wedding dress. It's white and floor-length with puffy bell-shaped sleeves. When I tried it on and looked in the mirror, I didn't even look like me!

As Mom was paying for my new formal, the clerk pointed out a hidden feature. "Look here," she said, "this gown has a lined pocket to hold the necessities—a compact, aspirin, a handkerchief, even one of those tiny lipsticks."

Mom and I both laughed at the idea of all that extra baggage. I told her that I'd rather carry

sliced carrots or sugar cubes in the secret pocket than all that other stuff! Then on the long drive home, she tried to impress on me the importance of being a "lady." I'm not sure this is going to be fun.

But I faced a much bigger worry. *What* can we do about Brown Sunshine's sad tail? It looks horrible, almost ratty! Especially when the rest of him is so handsome.

I out and out asked Freddy Westover. For once he didn't even snicker.

"No problem," he said. "Howd'ya like to borrow a false tail?"

"From where?"

"From my equipment for my show horses."

I couldn't believe it could be that simple. But it was! When we put on his false tail, it perfectly matched Brown Sunshine's coat. He swished his new tail with abandon, as if it felt good and belonged to him.

CHAPTER 18

SPRING SHOW
MULE CLIP

Molly felt sorry for anyone who wasn't "behind the scenes" with Brown Sunshine on the day before his crowning. After she gave the mule a bath, her father was ready to give him a clean shave called a Spring Show Mule Clip. Mr. Moore was Sunshine's barber, with the advice of Joe Henry Covington. With his thumb, Mr. Moore tested the sharpness of the buzzing clipper he was ready to use.

Brown Sunshine quivered in fear at the prospect. But he didn't pull away. His trust overcame his fear.

The talk was in monosyllables.

"Where should I begin, J.H.?" Mr. Moore asked.

"Start down his cheeks and down on his nose."

"Where then?"

"Shave twelve inches up from his chin, up to his neck."

Brown Sunshine was not happy with the talk nor with the noise of the clipper blade. For comfort, he licked a bit of salt from Mr. Moore's palm before he felt the tickle and heard  the buzzing of the razor traveling down his ears, leaving two tufts of hair on the very tips.

At last, it was over. Brown Sunshine was relieved, and pleased by the cool morning wind applauding the results. Mr. Moore rewarded his victim with a whole sugar cube, trying to make peace again between man and mule.

The next day, after Molly finished dressing in her long, white gown, Pops knocked at her bedroom door. He was holding something behind his back.

"Molly," he said, "I learned long ago, in a creative-writing class, that a good newspaper reporter can take notes during an interview without anyone noticing that he is writing. You can, too." He pressed a tiny diary into her hand. The small book had two handsome chestnut mules on the front cover and a small pencil tucked into the binding.

"Oh, Pops, I'll report the whole parade!" Molly said. "Now I'm ready!"

CHAPTER 19

MULE DAY

Dear Diary,

I've never ridden in a parade before. Especially a Mule Day Parade. You can't imagine the excitement of it. This bright red wagon with the yellow-spoked wheels is about to be pulled by two enormous Belgian draft mules. Brown Sunshine himself is standing tall in his reserved box, waiting, as if he knows that history is about to be made. He's almost the same height as Joe Henry Covington, who's sitting on the driver's bench wearing brand-new bibbed overalls and a grin that spreads ear to ear. Because he will be busy waving to the crowd, Mr. Covington's *not* doing the driving. John Robert Skillington, the famous driver of many Mule Day parades, *is!*

The excitement mounts. Three flags on our wagon snap in the breeze—the United States flag, the Maury County flag, and our Tennessee State flag. And banners on both sides of the wagon proclaim:

MR. JOE HENRY COVINGTON
GRAND MARSHAL

MR. JOHN ROBERT SKILLINGTON
HONORARY DRIVER

AND

<u>KING MULE</u>

BROWN SUNSHINE
OF SAWDUST VALLEY

CHAPTER 20

THE KING

Two whopper-size draft mules pulled Molly and Brown Sunshine's red wagon to the starting place: the regal Atheneum. The building looked untouchable with its intricate cutwork siding and wraparound porch. In the growing audience, Molly could see Mom and Pops waving to Brown Sunshine. They were proud of him, standing like a king, observing his attendants: The Queen and her Court of Five, including his delighted owner!

The Queen carried the glittering golden crown on a pillow of red velvet to match the King's red wagon. The band played "Seventy-Six Tron.bones" as she threaded her way through the narrow aisle of the float. When she

reached Brown Sunshine, a member of her Court quieted the band. The Queen stood on tiptoe to place the crown between the two magnificent shaved ears, bringing the elastic cords down his cheeks and fastening them with a strong bow-knot under his chin. Now Brown Sunshine's crown was a-glitter with rhinestones that looked like real diamonds and blue-green sapphires and red rubies—outshining every member of the court.

The crowd roared; the parade was about to start!

Entries surrounded Molly's wagon. Directly behind her was a wagon filled to the brim with tiptoe dancers, or cloggers. And among the whirling dancers was Molly's librarian, Elizabeth

Potts . . . the very one who had helped her with her essay.

Sharing the wagon with the cloggers was trick-roper Wimpy Jones, towering above his fellow passengers at six foot six. Wimpy tossed his lariat out over the crowd, carefully controlling the size of the loops so he didn't snag anyone in the audience.

Wagons with big and little floats continued to line up. An elegant all-gray hearse, drawn by two matching gray mules, pulled into the procession. The driver was a giant of a man, dressed in formal black with a wide black hat. The gray block of people bunched in the bed of the wagon were mourners. What more was there to know? Last year, the wagon and driver won the contest. This year, the judges were still deciding. But Molly didn't want to know! Neither did Brown Sunshine. He was making snuffling noises of delight.

The parade began to move. They were on their way! The King's float took the lead. Brown Sunshine carefully turned his crowned head to recognize a group of friends. They let out a wild cheer! And he replied with a loud bray, lifting his false tail as if every hair of it were his own.

The almost-noon sunshine shone like a spotlight above the bed of the wagon. And the King seemed to grow in height, in demeanor.

Long lines, mostly of mules, labored up the steep hill that winds through Columbia. The number of watchers doubled, tripled. People perched in trees, straddled housetops, and even climbed on each other's shoulders to get a closer view of Brown Sunshine and his Court and the famous driver, Skillington.

Buggies and carts and wagons followed, drawn by little cotton mules, large farm mules, still-larger sugar mules, and mammoth draft mules. Drivers were accompanied by office-seekers from city and state and, as they rounded a bend in the road, by a cluster of kids eating ice-cream cones. The melting chocolate drizzled down their hands. Brown Sunshine perked up, swinging his head in the direction of the kids. He stretched out toward the ice cream, slavering. But Molly quickly reached

into her pocket and offered him the sliced carrots she'd hidden there earlier. He wasted no time nuzzling her hand to find the warm, damp treat, and he kept licking, even after the carrots were long gone.

The two hours must have seemed endless to the pullers, but it passed quickly for Molly and the Court and the famous officials. They were busy waving and grinning to keep everyone happy.

At last they reached the fairgrounds, at the end
of the hill, and Molly slid her tiny diary into her
pocket. Everyone wanted to meet the proud King
and the beautiful young Queen who had crowned
the youngest King in the history of Mule Day,
and to shake hands with the one-armed Grand
Marshal and the famous Mr. Skillington. They all
shook lots of hands. Poor Mr. Covington nearly
got his one hand pumped off! Brown Sunshine

offered his right forefoot, "shaking hands" with the people who smelled familiar to him. Most of the visitors seemed to be strangers, but then they started shaking hands with each other!

Suddenly Freddy Westover popped out of the crowd. He shook hands with Mr. Covington and Mr. Skillington, and then turned, eyes skimming down the Queen's Court until they fixed on the last and youngest member.

"Molly!" he gasped, taking in her long gown. "Is it really you?"

She nodded, grinning, as Brown Sunshine lifted his forefoot to be shaken.

CHAPTER 21

HOME

As the crowd thinned to a few stragglers, Brown Sunshine suddenly felt his crown growing heavier on his head. Even the sparkle of the rhinestones seemed to be fading. And the wooden rails confining his body were like rulers, ready to slap. His tail seemed hampered, too, as if it knew that only half belonged to him.

Being a king was a one-day hurdle. The honors were packed into a few hours of beauty. It was as if he felt the brevity of his reign and was ready to go back to work.

Suddenly, the whole atmosphere changed. The red wagon was slithering its way out of the fairgrounds, letting swallows of new air flow over

Brown Sunshine. He could hear the mules pulling. He could feel the fresh air washing his face, trying to loosen the tight strings down his cheeks and the knot under his chin.

Even before Molly had planted a kiss on Brown Sunshine's forehead and left, Sunshine felt a new surge of life. He was home again . . . in his own paddock with his mother grazing nearby. He fell to his knees in the coolness of the grass, and then to his side. He was rubbed by the earth. He sniffed and rolled in contentment. Then he gave a full turn to his other side. He had never made a full turn before! Overhead he saw the deep blue sky holding a brilliant half-moon.

He squished back and forth, making full turns. He felt a strange new richness of life, as if he were just beginning to live it. He could hear Molly's faraway laughter, calling good-bye to folks and hello to "now." He snorted and let the sound fade in utter homefulness.

Molly peered from her bedroom window to see Sunshine rolling in his pasture. She smiled. Taking out her new diary, she wrote: Dear Diary,

Brown Sunshine has affected everyone's life for the good. Even Freddy Westover is looking taller and wiser, and more wonderful to me.

I'm glad Pops gave me this diary. Now we have a record of Sunshine's reign. I'll read it to him whenever I want him to remember how famous he was, and is, to be King for a Day. I wonder if he knows how much he is loved?

Somehow, I think he does!